For Wesley and Clara, my adventurers, and for my parents,
who made sure I played outside

TABLE OF CONTENTS

Chapter 1
READY TO ROUGH IT

Finley Flowers got her new hiking boots out of her closet and tugged them on. They were the color of rust, with thick, nubby soles, and they laced up her ankles like roller skates. They were dirt-kicking, trail-blazing, stump-stomping boots. She couldn't wait to try them out. It had only been a week since summer vacation had started, but it felt like a year. Now it was *finally* Finley's first day of overnight camp, and she was ready.

Finley tied her laces up tight and bounded down the stairs to the kitchen where her older brother,

Zack, was finishing a bowl of cereal. "I'm all packed for Camp Acorn!" Finley told him. "They have so many awesome activities — fishing, archery, camp cooking, creek exploring — there's even a raft on the lake where you can make cool crafts."

"I know," Zack said, putting his bowl in the sink. "I've been going there since I was eight, remember?" He threw a box of granola bars into his backpack. "Overnight camp's not all fun and games. You have to be tough to rough it."

"I'm tough." Finley stood tall. "Tougher than you."

"Ha!" Zack smirked. "We'll see about that."

Finley frowned. "What's that supposed to mean?"

"It means I'll believe it when I see it." Zack hoisted his backpack onto his shoulder and grabbed his sleeping bag. "Everyone knows boys are tougher than girls."

"They are not!" Finley protested.

Zack gave her a sly smile. "Prove it."

As he walked away, Finley's cheeks burned. Even though he was only two years older, Zack always made her feel small. But this time he'd gone too far. She'd show him how tough girls could be.

* * *

After breakfast, Finley lugged her bag to the car. Mom offered to help, but Finley shook her head. "I'm tough enough to carry my own stuff," she said.

Zack threw his pack in the backseat and flopped in after it. He turned up his headphones and took out his *Big League Boys* baseball book. Finley's little sister, Evie, climbed in beside him with her bag of snacks and magazines. Then they went to pick up Finley's best friend, Henry Lin. Finley was glad Henry was going to camp, too — it would be hard to spend a whole week without him.

When they pulled into Henry's driveway he was
sitting on his rolled-up sleeping bag, writing in his
notebook.

Probably checking his packing list, thought Finley.
Henry had a list for every situation.

After running to tell his mom and dad goodbye,
Henry chucked his things in the back of the car and
hopped in. "I just double-checked the list, and I'm all
set," he said.

Finley gave him a fist bump. "Camp Acorn, here we come!"

"Kate and Lia said they're going, too," said Henry. "It'll be just like school, but better."

Finley grinned. Kate and Lia were in Henry and Finley's class. They were always together, just like Finley and Henry.

The drive seemed to take forever. Evie whined about wanting to go to camp and sang "Ninety-Nine Bottles of Root Beer on the Wall" about a million times. Then she drank too many juice boxes, and they had to make three pit stops.

After a quick lunch at the Last Chance Diner — grilled cheese with extra pickles and a butterscotch-chocolate milkshake — Finley's carsickness kicked in. But Finley toughed it out — she didn't want to look like a baby in front of Zack.

Finally, they turned down a gravel lane, bumping and scraping along the road into the woods. It was dark in the shadows of the trees, except for a few beams of sunlight that cut through the dense canopy. Overgrown bushes scratched at the car windows.

"This forest is creepy," Evie said.

"Are you sure this is the right way?" Finley asked, hoping it wasn't. "It doesn't look like a camp."

"We're in the Whispering Woods," Mom said. "Listen! Nature's calling."

Finley listened, but all she could hear was the music buzzing from Zack's headphones like an annoying mosquito.

"Nature *is* calling," said Evie. "I've gotta go to the bathroom."

"Look!" Henry pointed to a weathered sign with the words "Camp Acorn" spelled out in log-like letters.

They veered right, and the woods opened up to a wide field bordered by a line of cabins. A bunch

of kids were playing Frisbee on the lawn. In the distance, the lake glinted silver in the afternoon sun.

"That's Lake Wannabe," said Mom.

"I *wanna be* swimming in it right now," said Henry.

Mom parked the car, and Finley leaped out. "Finally — fresh air!" She gave Mom a quick hug. "Okay, bye!"

"Wait a minute," Mom said. "You can't get rid of me that fast. We have to check in, and your stuff is still in the back."

"I'll meet you inside," Zack mumbled. "I want to finish this chapter."

Finley and Henry unloaded their bags and followed Mom and Evie to the camp office. Banners and T-shirts hung on the wall, and a glass case displayed mugs, bandannas, and other camp gear. While Evie went to the restroom, Finley and Henry checked out the photo wall — it was covered with pictures of kids swimming, roasting marshmallows, hiking, and doing all kinds of camp crafts.

Finley spotted a picture of Zack from last summer. He was standing on top of a boulder, posing like he'd just climbed Mt. Everest. Finley was so excited. She had longed to go to camp for two years, and now it was her turn. She was ready to rough it.

Chapter 2

WELCOME TO CAMP ACORN

Finley and Henry were studying the photos when a voice rang out from behind them. "Welcome to Camp Acorn!"

Finley spun around to face a woman with long, honey-colored hair and a wide smile. She was wearing a tie-dyed Camp Acorn T-shirt and a necklace with a mini dream-catcher charm.

"Greetings!" she said. "I'm Sunny Summers, camp director."

Is that her real name? Finley wondered as she shook Sunny's hand. "Finley Flowers," she said, "camper."

"Flowers," Sunny said. "You must be Zack's little sister."

Finley nodded. *Unfortunately*, she thought.

"And who is this?" Sunny turned to Henry.

"I'm Henry Lin," said Henry.

"Nice to meet you, Finley and Henry," Sunny said. "You're both in the Acorn group."

As Mom filled out some paperwork, Zack ambled in.

"Look who's a Sapling this year," said Sunny. "And a tall one, too. You must have grown a foot since last summer." She handed him a folder. "I think all your buddies are down by the dock."

"Thanks!" Zack turned to Mom and Evie. "Bye, guys. Don't miss me too much." He gave them each a quick hug, then bolted to look for his friends.

Sunny passed Finley and Henry their folders. "Inside you'll find your schedules with the activities you signed up for and some copies of the Camp Acorn map," she said.

"Cool!" Finley exclaimed, flipping through her folder.

"You're in the Lakeview cabin," Sunny told Henry, "the last one in the row. Seth is your cabin counselor. Finley, you're in the Treetop cabin with Zoey. It's the third one down. Get settled, then come hang out on the field. We'll have a Greeting Meeting at the fire pit at one o'clock. Then it's on to our afternoon activities."

Mom and Evie took Finley and Henry to drop off their stuff. They followed the wide path that ran in front of the row of red-roofed cabins. Finley pointed to the third one down. "There it is," she said. "Treetop!"

"Cute!" said Evie. "It's like a mini log cabin."

"Look at the view," Mom said, pointing to the lake in the distance.

Finley pushed the door open, and they stepped into a musty room.

"Oooh!" Evie said. "Bunk beds! *Lucky!*"

"Too bad all of the top ones are taken," Finley said, looking around. She threw her bag on the only empty bottom bunk. The bed above it was piled high with pillows, bags, and a whole zoo of stuffed animals.

Whoa, Finley thought. *Someone doesn't pack light.*

* * *

After they went to Henry's cabin to drop off his things, Mom glanced at her watch. "All right," she said. "Time to go. We'll walk you to the field and head home."

By the time they got there, the field was getting busy. Some of the older campers were playing soccer with the counselors. Others were practicing cartwheels and handstands or sitting in groups on the grass. Finley spotted Kate and Lia throwing a Frisbee down by the camp office. "Bye!" she said, giving Mom and Evie hugs. "I'll see you on Sunday!" Then she and Henry ran to join them.

"You're here!" Lia said.

Finley grinned. "Finally!"

"Olivia's here, too," said Kate, looking over her shoulder. "Her parents made her come. She went to her cabin to unpack her stuff."

"Which might take a while," Lia added, "since she has five bags."

Henry rolled his eyes. "Only five?"

Olivia Snotham drove Finley bonkers. She always had to be the best at everything and have everything her way — perfect.

Camp will be different, Finley thought. *There's no way Olivia will pick the same activities as me. She'll probably stay in her cabin and paint her nails.*

"What activities did you guys sign up for?" Lia asked.

Henry checked his folder. "Today I have fishing."

As they compared schedules, Olivia sashayed over. She was wearing patent leather sandals, oversized movie-star sunglasses, and a floppy sunhat, all in shades of purple.

"Did you get your stuff unpacked?" Kate asked her.

"No," Olivia said in her snippety voice. "I dumped my bags in the cabin and went to the office to call home. Somehow I forgot my hair dryer *and* my phone. I should be at my grandma's instead of this dumb camp. But Mom and Dad thought it would be *good* for me. Grandma's picking me up on Saturday. *If* I survive." She peered over the top of her sunglasses at Finley and Henry. "Anybody going to drama-rama?"

"Nope," said Henry.

Finley looked at her schedule and breathed a sigh of relief. "I've got camp crafts on the Craft Raft," she said.

Just then, Henry's watch beeped. "Time for the Greeting Meeting," he said. "I set my alarm so we wouldn't be late."

Finley and her friends followed some older kids and counselors to the campfire circle by the lake. Finley took a seat on one of the long benches, and Olivia and Henry sat down beside her. As campers drifted across the lawn, Finley spotted Zack and his buddies laughing and playing keep-away with a football. Finley scooted away from Olivia. She didn't want to be seen sitting with the Purple Princess.

When everyone was assembled, Sunny introduced herself and Doc, the assistant camp director. "It's great to look around and see all the smiling faces, old and new!" she said. "Before we start, I have a couple of announcements. We have tons of fun events planned, including the Camp Acorn Crawdad Derby on Wednesday, overnight campouts, and Field Day later in the week. Check the message board by the office so you know what's up. This year we're also having a weeklong scavenger hunt. You'll be collecting keepsakes from camp — things you find or make to remind you of your time here. At the end of the week, you'll put them in these memory jars for souvenirs." Sunny held up a glass jar for everyone to see.

"You already have your schedules," Doc said. "The activities you signed up for are in the mornings, and starting tomorrow there's a block of Free-to-Be time in the afternoons with free-choice activities. As I'm sure you know, there are three age groups at Camp Acorn — Acorns are the youngest, then Seedlings, then Saplings. On the front of your folder, there's a sticker to remind you what group you're in. We'll have some camp-wide events, but otherwise, please stay with your groups."

Doc looked around the circle and rubbed his hands together. "Now it's time for the fun part! On this first day of camp, there are assigned afternoon activities instead of Free-to-Be time, so listen for the activity you signed up for, and follow your counselors. Let's send the Acorns out first. Sylvie, do you want to start?"

A counselor with long braids, dangly earrings that looked like feathered lures, and a shirt that said "I ♥ FISHING" stepped into the circle. "Who's ready to fish?" she yelled, holding up a tackle box.

"That's me." Henry jumped to his feet and joined the small group of campers following Sylvie toward the lake.

"Good luck!" Finley called. "Catch a big one!"

Next, a young woman wearing paint-splattered, patch-covered denim shorts stood up. Even before she introduced herself, Finley guessed she had to be the camp crafts counselor.

"Attention, crafty campers!" she hollered. "My name is Zoey! This way to the Craft Raft — today we'll be knitting!"

Yay! thought Finley. *I've always wanted to learn to knit.*

As Finley got up, she glanced over at Zack. From across the circle, she could see him smirking.

"Have fun, knit-wit!" Zack said as she walked past. "Don't pull a muscle."

Suddenly, Finley wished she'd picked a more rugged activity. But she held her head high. Who said knitting couldn't be tough?

Chapter 3

HOME SWEET HOME-
AWAY-FROM-HOME

Finley and the other camp crafts campers followed Zoey down a trail by the edge of the lake and clomped along a skinny dock to a floating gazebo. Once everyone had found a spot on the floor, Zoey opened a chest of craft supplies and pulled out a plastic bin full of yarn.

"Pick a color," she said, "any color."

Finley chose a multicolored ball of yarn in shades of pink and orange. "I'm going to knit a hammock," she said.

"Let's start simple," Zoey said, smiling. "Our first project is going to be a coaster."

Finley frowned. "But that's boring!"

"Maybe you can use it as a hammock for a doll," Zoey suggested.

Zack would love that, Finley thought. She could already picture him making fun of her. *I'll pass on the doll hammock,* she decided. Besides, she had a better idea. She was going to knit something Fin-tastic.

Knitting *was* tough — way tougher than Finley had figured. At first, the yarn got tangled and the stitches kept falling off the needles. But Finley finally got the hang of it. As Zoey said, "Knitters aren't quitters."

When they had finished knitting, Zoey pulled out some other bins of art materials. Finley went straight for the modeling clay. It came in all kinds of cool colors — even neon and glow-in-the-dark. She ripped off some pieces of clay and started making tiny cups for a fairy tea set. But then she thought about what Zack might say and turned them into ninja throwing stars instead.

Finley loved the Craft Raft. She liked listening to the sound of the lapping water as she worked and feeling the gentle rocking of the raft tugging against its tether. Before she knew it, the session was over, and it was time for dinner.

Finley caught up to Henry at the picnic tables. "How was fishing?" she asked.

"I'm making a list of the fish I catch," Henry said. "But so far there's nothing on it. What did you make at the Craft Raft?"

"A ninja mask that turns into a slingshot!" Finley said, slipping it on. "How do I look?"

"Stealthy." Henry grinned. "Way to use your Flower Power." That was what he called the idea garden in Finley's head that was always sprouting Fin-ny thoughts.

"Thanks," Finley said. "I made some ninja stars to go with it, but Zoey still has to bake them so they'll harden. I'm going to make you something, too."

"Sweet!" said Henry. "I'll add it to my collection."

* * *

After dinner, Finley went to her cabin to unpack. Even from a distance, could tell something was different. As she got closer, she noticed the poofy lavender bow over the front door. Her stomach sank. This was *not* a tough-looking cabin. It was a purple palace. She glanced around to make sure Zack wasn't watching before she slipped inside.

Olivia was kneeling on the bunk above Finley's, tacking tinsel and fake flowers to the ceiling. She was surrounded by a mountain of plush purple blankets, pillows, and stuffed animals. The sharp aroma of nail polish hung in the air.

"There," said Olivia, adjusting a plastic rose. "Home sweet home-away-from-home."

Finley froze. *"You're* on the top bunk?"

"Of course." Olivia smiled sweetly. "Come check out the view."

"No thanks," said Finley.

Olivia smirked. "Scared of heights?"

"No," Finley said. "I'm scared I'll get lost in that big pile of purple."

* * *

That night, Finley couldn't get to sleep. Every time Olivia rolled over, the upper bunk sagged and creaked. Finley worried it might collapse from the weight of Olivia's accessories. And the fake-nature sounds from Olivia's noisemaker roared in Finley's ears, drowning out the lullabies of the real crickets.

Finley tried to think relaxing thoughts, but Olivia wormed her way into every single one. When she finally managed to fall asleep, Finley dreamed she was a fish swimming in Lake Wannabe. Olivia had hooked her with a glittery purple lure and was reeling her in.

Chapter 4
KNITTING NINJA

The next morning during camp crafts, Finley made some ninja nunchuks out of modeling clay and leather cord and started working on a top-secret project for Henry. Then she put on her ninja mask and went on a mission to the restroom. On the way back, she spotted a group of Sapling girls and boys, including Zack. She hid behind a tree to spy on them. They were sitting in a circle, whittling.

Finley wanted to whittle. She'd asked Zoey, but Zoey had said no. "If Acorns whittle, they might cut their fingers off," she'd told Finley.

As Finley snuck a glance from her hiding place, Zack looked up. Finley quickly ducked behind the tree. The next time she peeked out, he was standing right there.

"What are you doing?" Zack said. "Spying on me? And what's with that thing on your head?"

"I'm trying out my ninja mask," Finley said. "It doubles as a slingshot." She pulled off her mask, fired an acorn at a nearby tree, and missed.

"Ninjas don't use slingshots," said Zack. "And they *don't* wear pink masks."

"Well, they should," Finley told him.

Zack smirked. "Who knew knitting could be so exciting?"

"It's not just for grannies," said Finley, putting her mask back on.

"Well, have fun, and be careful with those knitting needles — they could poke your eye out," Zack said with a laugh.

Finley glared at Zack's back as he walked away. She loaded her slingshot and took aim, but he was already out of range. Besides, she didn't want to waste a perfectly good acorn.

* * *

Finley wore her ninja mask to lunch.

"That's an interesting look," said Olivia, sitting down at the picnic table beside Finley.

"*Fin*-teresting," Finley corrected.

"Can I see?" Lia asked.

Finley slipped off the mask and passed it to Lia.

"Here," said Olivia, pulling some daisy crowns out of her giant, purple purse. "Try these. I made them in nature study." She plunked them on Finley's head right as Zack walked by with a huge plate of cookies.

"Hey, little sis," he said, cramming one into his mouth. "Playing dress-up again? What happened to the Knitting Ninja?"

Finley scowled at her brother and yanked off the flower crowns. Why did he always have to appear at the worst times? She was never going to be able to prove she was tough.

"What's his problem?" Olivia asked as Zack walked away. "There's nothing wrong with playing dress-up."

Just then Henry slid onto the bench. "What's wrong?" he asked Finley. "You look kind of droopy."

Finley sighed. "Zack's tormenting me as usual. And it's totally unfair that the Saplings get to whittle, and we don't. Doesn't that bother you?"

Henry shrugged. "Maybe a *whittle*. What bothers me more is that there are six species of fish in Lake Wannabe, and I haven't caught a single one. Yesterday, Sylvie got two bass, and this boy named Simon got a sunfish. But me? Nothing. Not even a minnow."

"Maybe you can catch a crawdad," said Finley. "Tomorrow's the Crawdad Derby — I saw it on the message board. And Free-to-Be time is right before it. We can hike to the creek and catch crawdads for the contest."

"Sounds like a plan," Henry said.

I'm going to find the fastest crawdad at Camp Acorn, Finley thought, *so I can race against Zack and win.*

Chapter 5
LIGHTNING LEGS

The next day during Free-to-Be time, Henry's cabin counselor, Seth, offered to take a group of Acorns to catch crawdads. Finley, Henry, Kate, and Lia ran to get their water shoes.

"I'll come," Olivia said. "But I'm *not* getting wet."

Good luck with that, Finley thought.

"Today we're going to the awesome-est, top-secret-est crawdad-catching hole in the county," Seth said, handing Henry a bucket to carry the critters.

Finley and her friends followed Seth down the trail, winding past waterfalls and still pools and finally stopping at a wide part of the creek. Seth took off his hat and brushed back his shaggy bangs. "The best place to hunt for crawdads — also known as mudbugs — is where they like to hide." He lifted a large, flat rock, and something scuttled back, clouding the water. "There's one!" he said to Olivia. "Wanna catch it?"

"No thanks," said Olivia, wrinkling her nose.

"Don't you want a crawdad for the derby?" Seth asked.

Olivia shrugged. "What do you get if you win?"

"The glory of having the fastest crawdad, of course," he replied. "*And* the Golden Crawdad trophy."

"A trophy?" Olivia's eyes lit up. "Is it *real* gold?"

Seth laughed. "No, but it is a *real* crawdad shell spray-painted gold."

"Cool!" said Kate.

"Ew," said Olivia.

Just then Finley spotted something in the shallows. It looked like a miniature lobster. "Found one!" she said, lunging for it. The crawdad darted toward a crevice, pedaling its feet like a wind-up toy.

"Grab it from behind!" Seth coached.

Finley picked the crawdad up by its back. It wriggled and waved its claws, but Finley held on. "I'm going to call her Lightning Legs," she said. "Look at her go!"

"Hey, there's mine!" Henry pointed to a plump crawdad snuggled into the mud. He plucked it up gingerly and admired its long tail. "Finally, I caught something!"

"It didn't even try to get away," said Lia.

Henry stared into its stalky eyes. "I think I'll call him Stan," he said.

Seth helped Kate catch her crawdad next. She held it out to Henry's. "Stan, meet Nike," Kate said proudly. "Named after the Greek goddess of victory. And my sneakers."

"And this is Craw-Daddy," Lia said, picking up one with a silvery tail.

"I think it might be Craw-*Mommy*," Henry said. "My fishing book says the females have smaller claws."

"Craw-Mama then," said Lia. "I like the way that sounds."

Finley and Henry put water and rocks in the bucket to carry their crawdads back to camp. "There," Finley said. "It's a cozy little crawdad fort."

Seth glanced at his watch. "We'd better head back. The derby will be starting soon." He turned to Olivia. "Last chance to catch your very own mudbug."

"I'll pass," said Olivia.

"Come on," said Finley, holding Lightning Legs out to her. "You can't enter the derby without one."

"I don't *want* to enter the derby," Olivia snapped, backing away. Suddenly, she slipped on the wet rocks and landed in the creek.

"Uh-oh," Henry muttered. "Gravity strikes again."

"Are you okay?" Seth asked, offering her a hand.

Olivia sat there for a moment, her mouth hanging open. Then she scrambled to her feet. "My favorite dress — it's ruined!" She scowled at Finley.

"Don't look at me," Finley said. "It's not my fault. Those shoes don't have any treads."

Olivia frowned at her soggy sandals. "Great. They're ruined, too."

"Just let them dry out," Seth said. "They'll be as good as new."

Finley, Henry, Kate, and Lia put their crawdads in the bucket and took turns carrying it back to camp. Olivia trudged behind them the whole way back, her dripping dress clinging to her legs and her shoes squeaking.

* * *

By the time they arrived, counselors and campers were already gathering around a long row of folding tables. The tabletops had been painted with red and white targets, and a big orange bucket sat on top of each one.

"This way to the Crawdad Derby!" Doc called, waving them over. "If this is your first time here, you're in for a treat."

He held one of the buckets up to show that the bottom had been cut out. "We're going to place these buckets at the center of each table and drop the crawdads in. When the race starts, we'll lift the buckets, and the first crawdad to crawl to the edge of the target wins. The winner from each table will advance to the final race."

Finley spotted Zack standing at the last table. *All right, Lightning,* she thought. *Let's take this race by storm.*

Henry, Lia, and Kate picked up their competitors. Craw-Mama and Nike waved their pincers and fanned their tails. Stan just stared.

"You sure know how to pick 'em," Olivia said.

"He's saving his energy for the race," said Henry.

"All right, crawdad jockeys," Doc said, handing out numbered stickers. "Put one of these on your crawdad's back so we can tell who's who, then drop 'em in!"

Campers crowded closer to the tables. A short, red-haired boy squeezed in beside Finley and plopped his crawdad into the bucket. Henry, Kate, and Lia put theirs in, too.

Finley glanced over at Zack's table again. She couldn't wait for him to see Lightning in action. She stuck a number seven onto her crawdad's back. "Lightning," she said, "you're going to win this in a flash!" Then she leaned over and placed her in the bucket.

"These little fellers are ready to race!" Doc yelled. "Let's kick off the Forty-Fifth Annual Camp Acorn Crawdad Derby by hollering 'Peace, love, and crawdads!' On your marks . . . get set . . ."

"PEACE, LOVE, AND CRAWDADS!" everyone screamed.

When Doc lifted the bucket, the crawdads were a squirming mass of spiny legs and tails. "Look at that!" he shouted. "They're a lively bunch!"

"Ugh," said Henry. "It's making me *craws*trophobic."

Slowly, the crawdads spread out from the center of the target.

"Stan's just sitting there," said Olivia.

Kate leaned in for a closer look. "I think he might be dead."

"He's not dead," said Henry. "Wait till he decides to bust a move. Let's go, Stan, make it snappy! Get it — *snappy*?" He pinched his fingers together like claws, and Stan waved an antenna in his direction.

"Yay, Craw-Mama!" Lia clapped her hands as her crawdad struggled toward the outer circle.

"Lightning Legs is pulling into the lead!" Finley shrieked. But just then, her crawdad flipped over and turned around. "No, no, ding-a-ling! Other way!"

"Looks like she's going nowhere fast," said Olivia.

"Yes!" Kate screeched. "Nike's catching up!"

Just then the smallest crawdad broke away from the pack and scooted across the finish line.

"Yay, Rocket!" the red-haired boy cheered.

"We have a winner over at table one!" Doc announced.

Henry picked up Stan, who still hadn't moved. "It's okay, buddy," he said. "Maybe racing's not your thing."

Finley glanced at Zack, and her heart sank. His race was finished, too, and by the smug smile on his face, she could tell he'd won. He caught her looking and strutted over. "So," he said, "how'd it go?"

"She lost," Olivia reported.

"Aw, too bad," Zack said. "Come watch the final race — I'll show you how it's done."

But Finley didn't want to watch. She knew Zack would win, and she didn't want to hear his bragging. "Come on, Lightning," she said, peeling off the racing number and plopping her crawdad back into the bucket. "Time to bolt."

* * *

After the races, Finley and Henry volunteered to take the crawdads back to the creek. As they hiked to the crawdad-catching hole, the bucket bumped and sloshed against Finley's legs.

"Careful," Henry said. "Stan'll get seasick."

"Hang in there, Stan," said Finley. "We're almost home."

"I'm going to miss him," Henry said. "What if he's lonely?"

"He'll be okay," Finley said. "He's got Lightning Legs. Besides, we can always come visit."

When they reached the creek, Finley tipped the bucket, and the crawdads drifted out. "Swim!" she said, as they dashed to the shadows. "Be free!"

Chapter 6
TENT FOR TWO

The next morning at breakfast, Olivia's eyes lit up. "Who needs creepy-crawly crawdads?" she said, pointing to a chipmunk perched on a nearby trashcan. "I'm going to tame *that* cute critter and keep it as a pet." She held out a piece of her chocolate-chip granola bar and made kissy noises with her mouth.

The chipmunk stood up on its hind legs, ears twitching.

"He's so precious," Olivia cooed. "I've always wanted a chinchilla, but my mom won't let me get one. A chipmunk could work."

Henry raised an eyebrow. "Chipmunks are rodents, and rodents carry diseases. Ever hear of *the plague?*"

"Don't be ridiculous," Olivia said. "Is that a face that wants to spread the plague? I don't think so. All it wants is some love."

Henry shook his head. "All it wants is your breakfast."

Olivia crept closer. "Aw, come here, you chubby-cheeked little rascal. Look at your racing stripes — I think I'll call you Speedy."

"Remember the sign about not feeding wild critters?" Henry said. "Speedy is wild."

"Besides, the chocolate chips might make him sick," said Finley.

Olivia shoved the last bite of bar into her mouth, and the chipmunk scurried away.

Just then Doc stood up, and Sunny blew her whistle. "Listen up, Acorns," Doc said. "We have an announcement. Today the Seedlings and Saplings leave for their campouts. Tomorrow *you'll* have your first overnight campout."

Yes! thought Finley. *My chance to demonstrate my Fin-omenal outdoor skills!*

"We'll be taking a bus to the other side of the Whispering Woods to do some rustic camping," Sunny said. "Treetop and Hillcrest cabins will go with Zoey and me to the Blackberry Campsite, and Creekside and Lakeview cabins will go to the Magnolia Campsite with Seth and Doc."

"Rustic?" interrupted Olivia. "Does that mean there's no electricity in the cabins?"

Sunny gave her a patient smile. "It means there are *no* cabins — you'll be sharing a tent with your bunkmate."

Olivia looked like she'd rather eat worms. She glanced over at Finley.

No, Finley thought. *This can't be happening. It's the ultimate toughness test, and I'm paired with Princess Perfect.*

* * *

After breakfast, Finley, Henry, and Kate went to archery for their morning activity.

"Look," Kate said, "I'm Artemis, Goddess of the Hunt." She shot an arrow at the target for ten points.

"Nice!" said Henry.

"I'm Robin Hood!" Finley hollered. She pulled back an arrow and let it fly. "Oops!" she said, as it glanced off a nearby tree and landed at the archery counselor's feet.

Henry got three bull's-eyes in a row and finished with the highest score in the group.

Finley had hoped she'd become a Camp Acorn archery legend so she could brag about it to Zack when he got back. But the only bull's-eye she got was on the next target over, and she was pretty sure that didn't count.

* * *

At dinner, Olivia plunked her tray down across from Finley and Henry. Her cheeks and nose were watermelon pink.

"Hoo-boy," said Henry. "What happened to your face?"

"Duh," said Olivia. "It's called a sunburn. I had swimming, and I forgot my sunscreen."

Henry shielded his eyes. "It looks like you're glowing."

"It *feels* like I'm glowing," Olivia said, pouting.

Henry pulled a plastic bag out of his backpack. "Here, have some gorp."

"Excuse me?" said Olivia.

"*Gorp,*" said Henry. "Also known as trail mix." He took some foil packets out of the bag and handed them to Finley and Olivia. "We made it yesterday in camp cooking."

"It looks like birdseed," Olivia said, unwrapping it.

"It's Good Old Raisins and Peanuts — G-O-R-P," Henry explained, "but we added some granola and chocolate chips."

Finley sampled some. "Mmm," she said, "G-O-R-P is G-O-O-D."

Olivia picked out the chocolate chips and ate them, then folded up the packet and put it in her purse. "I think I'll save the rest for later," she said, smiling politely. Then she spotted Speedy by the trashcans and started in with her chipmunk chatter.

She tore off a piece of hotdog bun and threw it in his direction.

Henry plugged his ears. "Enough chirping already. Who knows what you're saying in chipmunk-ese? You could be telling it to attack."

Speedy darted in and grabbed the bun, then scampered off.

"Quit being so negative," said Olivia. "He senses your tension."

"Speaking of *tent*-ion, I can't wait for our campout tomorrow," Henry said.

"It's going to be awesome!" said Finley. "Just a thin layer of fabric between us and the great outdoors."

Olivia shook her head. "It doesn't *sound* awesome. It sounds like torture."

"We'll be like pioneers on the wild frontier," said Henry. "Like cowhands on the open range. Like —"

"Like kids on a campout wishing they had a widescreen TV and a real bed?" said Olivia. "At least I have my disco headlamp. Maybe we can have a spa night in the tent. I just got some new Party Purple nail polish."

Finley sighed. Sharing a tent with Olivia just might be the toughest thing she'd do all week.

* * *

After dinner, Finley went to the Craft Raft with Zoey to pick out more yarn for her special project so she could work on it during evening quiet time. She was on her way back to the cabin when she found Olivia sprinkling gorp on the trail. Finley stood in the middle of the path and waited until Olivia backed right into her.

"Aaagh!" Olivia yelped. "What are you doing?"

"*I'm* going to the cabin to get ready for the campout," said Finley. "What are *you* doing?"

Olivia crossed her arms. "Making a trail."

Finley raised her eyebrows. "That's not why they call it *trail* mix. This wouldn't have anything to do with a squeaky little furball named Speedy, would it?"

"I'm leaving him a snack," Olivia said. "Is that such a crime?"

Finley sighed. "What are you going to do when Speedy follows your trail into our cabin?"

"Keep him," said Olivia. "I think he likes me."

Finley shook her head. "He's a *wild animal*. He only likes you for your gorp. Besides, Zoey will never let you keep him."

"Zoey will love him," said Olivia. "He'll be the perfect cabin mascot."

Finley gave up and went to the cabin to pack. She checked her list: sleeping bag, sleep mat, pajamas, toiletry kit, bug spray, flashlight, book. Then she set out her hiking boots.

Time to break you in, Finley thought. *Nature calls.*

Chapter 7

DOOON'T FEEED THE CHIPMUUUNKSSSSS . . .

The next afternoon, the Acorns boarded the
Camp Acorn Express — a beat-up school bus with a
rainbow painted on the side. Sunny and Doc led the
sing-along as they bounced down the rutted road,
shouting over the roar of the engine. "Down by the
banks of the Hanky Panky where the bullfrogs jump
from bank to banky, with an eeps, ipes, opes, opps,
one fell in and went kerplops!"

They were halfway through "This Land is Your Land" when the bus wheezed and lurched to a stop. Finley slung her backpack over her shoulder and filed down the aisle with the rest of the campers.

"All right, Treetop and Hillcrest campers," Sunny called once they'd all gathered outside, "this way to the Blackberry Campsite!"

As they started down the trail, Finley waved goodbye to Henry.

"Good luck!" he called, waving back.

Finley's group followed Sunny and Zoey to a clearing in the woods. By the time they got there, Finley was ready to take off her pack and relax.

Sunny and Zoey demonstrated how to set up a two-person tent, then passed out tents to every pair of bunkmates.

"Pick a spot and get set up," said Sunny. "Make yourselves comfortable."

Finley and Olivia were the last ones to set up their tent. First Olivia had to find a perfectly level spot. Then they couldn't agree on which direction the flap should face. When they'd finally figured out the puzzle of poles and pockets, Olivia insisted on decorating their home-away-from-home-away-from-home with fake flowers and ribbons.

By the time they'd unrolled their sleeping bags, the other campers were exploring the campground

and collecting firewood. Olivia dug in her purse and pulled out her headlamp. She slipped it on and pressed a button on the side. Suddenly, the tent was a kaleidoscope of color.

"Yikes!" Finley exclaimed, shielding her eyes from the pulsing rainbows.

"I really wish I'd brought my karaoke machine," said Olivia.

I'm really glad you didn't, thought Finley.

"I guess that wouldn't exactly be roughing it, though," Olivia added.

"You're not exactly roughing it now," Finley said. "You've got a disco headlamp, plastic flowers, and an inflatable mattress that's two feet thick."

"Yeah, but I'm sleeping in a tent," said Olivia. "What about that?"

Finley shrugged. "It's not *real* camping unless you sleep under the stars."

Olivia frowned. "Fine." She wrestled her air mattress out the tent door and came back for her sleeping bag and her mountain of poofy pillows and blankets. "Where's *your* stuff?" she asked. "You're sleeping out here, too, right?"

"Of course," said Finley. She dragged her mat and sleeping bag outside and set them up on the other side of the tent.

"Girls!" Zoey called. "Come help build a campfire so we can start dinner!"

Once all the campers had collected their sticks, Sunny showed them how to lean them together like a tepee over a pile of twigs and pinecones. She lit the twigs and blew gently, and they burst into flames. Then she added some split logs, and the fire climbed higher.

Finley was famished. Sunny's campfire chili hit the spot. The garlic bread was burned, but Finley didn't care. "Camping out sure makes you hungry," she said, helping herself to seconds while Olivia picked at her food.

When the girls were done with dinner, Zoey got out some marshmallows. "Who wants s'mores?"

"Me!" everyone screamed, running to find roasting sticks.

Zoey passed out marshmallows, and the girls speared them with the sticks and gathered around the fire. Olivia held her marshmallow high above the gently glowing coals, turning and inspecting it every two seconds. "I like mine golden brown," she said. "This one's going to be perfect."

Finley put her marshmallow straight into the fire and kept it there till it bubbled and burst into flames. "I like mine well-done," she said.

Finley held the melting marshmallow up like a torch and blew it out. Then she sandwiched it between two graham crackers and tucked in a slab of chocolate. Sticky, sweet goo oozed out the edges.

"Mmm . . ." she said, taking a bite. "The taste of the great outdoors."

"How about some campfire songs?" Sunny suggested as the sun sank below the ridge.

"I'd rather tell ghost stories!" Kate said spookily.

"Yeah!" echoed the other girls.

"Finley, you go first," said Kate, the glow from the fire reflecting on her face. "You're creative. Let's see what scary story you can make up."

"Finley's good at making scary stuff," said Olivia. "Remember her school cook-off creation?"

Finley glared at Olivia. Maybe a spooky story was just what she needed to toughen her up. But Finley had to think fast. Looking around, she spotted an old, peeling "Don't Feed the Critters" sign by the trail. *Perfect*, she thought.

Finley took a swig of water. "All right," she said in her most serious voice. "This is a really scary story

because it's true. It's about a girl who was camping right here, at the Blackberry Campsite. At that time, this camp was known as Camp Chuck-A-Chick."

"That's a silly name for a camp," said Olivia. "No wonder they changed it."

Finley ignored her. "Some folks say it was named after the sound chipmunks make," she continued. "Anyway, there was this fifth-grade girl, Josie, who loved animals, especially the cute and cuddly kind."

Olivia narrowed her eyes at Finley. "What is this story about?"

"A girl and a chipmunk," Finley said. "Only *this* chipmunk wasn't like other chipmunks, because . . . " She lowered her voice to a whisper. "It was a *vampire* chipmunk."

Olivia snorted. "That's ridiculous. There's no such thing as a vampire chipmunk. Chipmunks are adorable."

"That's *exactly* what Josie thought," Finley said. "One day, as she and her friends were heading to the fire pit, they realized they'd forgotten the marshmallows. Josie was on her way back from getting them when she heard a noise — *CHUK-A-CHICK. CHICK-CHIIICK.*"

Finley paused and looked around the campfire circle. Everyone was spellbound, including Olivia.

"Josie looked up and saw a cute chipmunk perched on the branch of a nearby tree," Finley said. "She stopped to watch it, and it watched her back with its beady little eyes. Suddenly, it occurred to Josie that the little guy might be hungry. She'd read the signs about not feeding the critters, but she figured one little marshmallow couldn't hurt. It didn't take her long to coax the chipmunk closer. *CHIIICK-A-CHUCK. CHUCK-CHIIICK.* Josie held out her hand. But instead of grabbing the marshmallow, the chipmunk sank its fangs into her finger. Before she could scream, it was all over."

"What happened?" Kate asked, her eyes wide.

Finley glanced around the circle mysteriously. "No one knows for sure. They found the bag of marshmallows on the trail. But Josie was never seen again. They say that same vampire chipmunk still wanders these woods, and on nights when the moon is full, if you listen closely, you can hear Josie's voice like a warning on the wind: *'Dooon't feeed the chipmuuunksssss . . .'*"

For a moment, everyone was silent. Then Olivia burst out laughing. "That's the dumbest ghost story I've ever heard."

Sunny shot her a stern look. "I thought it was very creative," she said.

Finley shrugged. "That's the way I heard it. They tried to trap the chipmunk, but they could never catch it. Eventually, they sold the camp, and the new owners changed the name to Camp Acorn."

"Yikes!" Lia said, pulling her blanket tighter around her shoulders.

"Vampire chipmunks," Olivia scoffed. "You guys are total dorks if you fall for that."

Finley glanced over at Olivia. Her voice sounded a little too loud — almost nervous. Olivia acted like she'd never believe some old ghost story. But Finley could tell that deep down she wasn't so sure.

Chapter 8
WHEN YOU GOTTA GO . . .

No one else could think of a ghost story to follow Finley's, so they decided to sing campfire songs instead. After a couple of rounds of "You Are My Sunshine," the fire was dying down, and Sunny and Zoey announced that it was tent time.

As soon as Finley stepped away from the fire pit, the mosquitoes moved in. "Run for your life!" she yelled, waving her arms around her head. "Vampire mosquitoes!"

Finley raced back to her tent and dove inside. She pulled on her pajamas, spritzed herself with bug spray, tucked her messy braids into the hood of her jacket, and tied the strings tight.

Olivia burst in a moment later. After changing into her pajamas, she put on a bug hat and pulled the mesh veil over her face. Then she wrapped herself up in a blanket of mosquito netting. "Mosquitoes love me," she said. "My mom says it's because I'm so sweet."

"Knock, knock," said a voice from outside.

Finley unzipped the door a crack and peeked out. It was Lia. "Sunny and Zoey are taking us to the nature center to brush our teeth," she said. "Are you coming?"

"We'll be right there," Finley replied, grabbing her toiletry kit and pulling on her ninja mask to use as a headband.

Finley and Olivia scrambled out of the tent and followed Lia to the edge of the campsite where the others were waiting.

"Ready for a night hike?" Zoey asked. "Once we're moving, the mosquitoes won't be so bad."

"Look," Kate said, pointing up at the sky. "It's a full moon."

"Just like in Finley's story," said Lia, shivering.

"This is the perfect place to stargaze," Sunny said as they started down the trail. "Without all those city lights getting in the way, we've got a pretty awesome view."

As they walked, Finley leaned her head back and scanned the sky. It was like someone had flicked a switch and turned on millions of Christmas lights. *Wow*, she thought. *In-Fin-ity. Who knew there were so many stars?* It was hard to believe they were right above her all the time.

Hiking seemed to take longer in the dark. The forest was full of nighttime noises — scurrying, scampering, hooting, croaking, and other unidentifiable sounds. Finley told herself there was nothing to be scared of, but she walked close to Zoey just in case.

After a while, the group turned off the main trail and took a narrow one that snaked through the tall trees. Eventually, they reached the nature center — a small brick building with a tin roof. When they stepped inside, the lights came on with a loud buzz.

"Finally!" Olivia gasped. "Civilization!"

The girls took turns brushing their teeth and refilling their water bottles. While they waited for Olivia to comb her hair, Finley examined her new crop of summer freckles. She hoped they brought good luck, like Mom always said. They were definitely multiplying.

By the time they got back to the campsite, Finley could barely keep her eyes open. Between the night noises and the monster mosquitoes, she was wishing she could cuddle up in a snug little cabin. Or at least the tent. But she was the one who'd suggested sleeping under the stars. She couldn't back out now. If word got back to Zack, he'd tease her about it forever.

"Sweet dreams," Zoey said as she headed for her tent.

"See you girls bright and early for a morning hike," Sunny said. "Goodnight."

"Goodnight," said Olivia, fluffing up her pillows. Then she disappeared under her sea of netting and blankets.

One night, Finley thought, tugging her ninja mask down over her ears. *I can do this.* She slid into her sleeping bag and pulled it over her head, leaving a tiny air hole. Listening to the bloodthirsty buzzing outside her cinched-up cocoon, she pictured her sleeping bag covered in a blanket of bugs.

Above the hungry humming, Finley heard all kinds of other sounds — chirping, trilling, hooting, and rustling. When nature called, it sure was noisy. And the snoring coming from the counselors' tent was louder than the Camp Acorn Express.

But then Finley heard a different sound. It was soft at first — so soft she thought it might not be there at all. As she strained to hear it, the noise got louder. It sounded sneaky. Like the barely there footsteps of someone — or some*thing* — trying not to be heard.

Finley crossed her fingers and held her breath. The vampire chipmunk wasn't real. She'd made it up herself, so how could it be? *Unless* she had some kind of special powers. Maybe she just *thought* she was making it up, but somehow, without knowing it, she was telling what had really happened. If there was a vampire chipmunk, it might have heard her . . . and it might be coming after her right now!

Suddenly, the sound stopped.

Finley felt a slow, rhythmic tapping on her head. She froze.

"Hey," a voice whispered. "Are you awake?"

It was Olivia.

Finley fumbled with the zipper on her sleeping bag and poked her head out. "*What?*" she whispered.

"I've gotta go to the bathroom," Olivia said. "*Bad.*"

From the look on her face, Finley could tell it was true. "Then go," she said, pointing to the trees. "Before the mosquitoes eat you alive."

Olivia peered into the woods. "I can't — there are ticks and snakes and worse in there. I need to use the real bathroom at the nature center."

"Are you kidding me?" said Finley. "You'll never make it."

"I can hold it," Olivia insisted. "I just need someone to go with me."

"Ask Sunny or Zoey. They'll go with you."

"No, they won't. They'll get all rustic and tell me to go in the woods." Olivia made her best puppy-dog face. "Maybe you could —"

Finley frowned. "No way."

Olivia clasped her hands together. "Pleasepleasepleasepleaseprettypleeeeeease?"

Finley shook her head. "No," she said. "Good luck. And watch out for the vampire chipmunk."

With that, Finley ducked her head back into her sleeping bag and zipped it up tight. After a minute she heard Olivia's footsteps fade. Finally, she could get some sleep. Except . . .

"*Great*," Finley muttered. "Now *I* have to go."

Chapter 9

DRACUMUNK

Finley wriggled out of her sleeping bag and slipped on her hiking boots. She tiptoed to the edge of the trail and glanced back at the campsite. In the moonlight, the tents looked like a peaceful village. The woods surrounding them seemed even darker than before.

The nature center isn't that far, Finley told herself. *I bet Zack wouldn't be scared to go.*

Taking a deep breath, Finley started down the trail. As she rounded a curve, she saw Olivia up ahead. "Hey," she whisper-called. "Wait!"

Olivia spun around. "Quit sneaking up on me like that!" she hissed, hoisting her purse onto her shoulder. "I thought you weren't coming."

"I changed my mind," said Finley, jogging to catch up.

Olivia held up her headlamp, which had gone dark. "My batteries ran out," she said. "But it's kind of pretty with the moonlight. You can even see your shadow." She pointed to the ground in front of them.

"Except in there," Finley said, nodding in the direction of the woods. "Who knows what lurks in *those* shadows . . ."

"Cut it out!" said Olivia, walking faster. "Let's just get to the bathrooms, do our thing, and get back." She gave Finley a nervous glance. "You don't think a chipmunk could chew through someone's clothing, do you?"

Finley shrugged. "Sure, if it really wanted to. Why?"

Olivia pulled her sweater up around her chin. "Just wondering."

The girls wound their way through the woods until they came to a fork in the trail.

"Everything looks so different at night," said Finley. "I think the nature center is that way." She pointed to the right.

"Are you sure?" Olivia asked, shifting her weight from foot to foot.

"Pretty sure," Finley said.

Suddenly, something rustled in the woods to their left.

"Let's *go*," Olivia whispered.

After a minute, the trail got twisty, and the trees seemed to close in.

"We better get there soon," Olivia said. "I don't know if I can hold it much longer."

Just then, Finley spotted a flicker of light up ahead. As they rounded a bend, the slanted roof of the nature center came into view.

"Boy, am I glad to see that," said Olivia.

When they opened the door, the lights clicked on, bathing the cinderblock walls with an artificial glow.

"Whew!" said Olivia, heading for the biggest stall.

Finley used one of the other stalls and then took an extra long time washing her hands. She didn't even complain when Olivia combed her hair. The bathroom felt safe and warm. But she knew they had to get back. *What if Sunny and Zoey wake up and wonder where we are?* she thought.

As Finley and Olivia stepped into the darkness and started down the trail, an owl called in the distance. *Ha-ha-hoo-hoooo!*

Olivia stopped short. "Hey, where did those come from?" she asked, pointing to several paths that split off from the one they were on.

Finley shrugged. "I guess we didn't see them when we were going the other way," she replied. "There are probably lots of different trails that lead to the nature center."

"I wish we had a flashlight that worked," said Olivia.

As they hiked, the trail started to climb up, up, up. Then it sloped gently downwards and curved to the left.

"I don't remember this part," Olivia said, her voice quivering.

Finley stopped. "Me neither. We should have brought a compass and a map."

"We should have brought a grown-up," said Olivia. "Now what do we do?"

"When you're lost you're supposed to stay put and let people find you," Finley said. "I read it in Henry's *How to Survive Pretty Much Anything* book."

Olivia shook her head. "But no one's even going to miss us until morning. I can't wait that long. Besides, something else might find us first."

Just then a twig snapped in the tangled brush nearby. Then another.

A shiver ran up Finley's back. *"Shhhh!"* She put her finger to her lips.

Olivia's eyes were as big as two full moons. "What is it?" she whispered.

"I don't know," said Finley. "But I think it's following us."

"Okay," said Olivia. "We are going to stay calm. There are lots of nocturnal animals that go about their business at night. They're probably more scared of us than we are of —"

CH-CH-CHUCK. CH-CHIIICK.

"No," Finley whispered, "they're not! Come on!" She grabbed Olivia's hand and took off running.

"Where are we going?" Olivia called as they barreled down the trail.

"Away from whatever's making that noise!" Finley shouted over her shoulder.

Finley and Olivia ran until they couldn't run anymore. The trail angled up again, and Finley stopped and leaned against a boulder to catch her breath. "Wait a minute," she said. "Didn't we pass that fallen tree before?"

"Oh, no!" Olivia cried. "We've been running in circles. We're lost!" Tears spilled down her cheeks. "Now we'll never be rescued, and the vampire chipmunk will track us down, and I'll never get to stay up late and eat my grandma's world-famous chocolate-mint brownies, or get a chinchilla, or go to Paris when I grow up!"

"Listen," Finley said, "we've got to stay calm. Let's sit down and have a drink and think."

"Okay," Olivia said shakily. She pulled her water bottle and some little tin cups out of her purse, then filled one and passed it to Finley.

"Thanks," Finley said, taking it. "Hey, what else is in there?"

Olivia rifled through her purse. "Let's see . . . a change of clothes, my toiletry kit, a picnic set my grandma gave me, a water gun, a pack of glow sticks, some purple duct tape for decorating emergencies —"

"I've got it!" Finley exclaimed. "Fin-spiration! Pass me the bowls and plates from the picnic set."

Olivia handed them over, and Finley turned one of the bowls upside down and placed it on Olivia's head. Then she ripped off some duct tape and made a chinstrap to hold it in place. "Helmets," she said, securing her own, "in case of attack from above."

Finley grabbed the picnic plates. "Now for the shields to fend off rampaging rodents." She attached duct-tape handles to the backs of the plates and passed one to Olivia.

"Thanks," Olivia said. "I feel better already."

"I wish I'd brought my throwing stars," Finley said, taking off her ninja-mask-slingshot and picking up some acorns to use as ammunition. She handed Olivia the water gun. "You'd better fill that up."

Olivia did.

"Got any of that white sunscreen?" Finley asked. "It'll make us look tough and help camouflage our scent."

"Good idea," Olivia agreed, pulling a tube out of her toiletry kit. "Plus, we might be too slippery to catch."

The girls slathered the greasy sunscreen all over their faces, and Finley rummaged through the purse again. "If only we had some kind of neck guards . . . wait a minute. What's this?" she asked, holding up a foil packet.

"Henry's gorp," said Olivia, looking guilty.

"You were saving it for Speedy, weren't you?" Finley sighed. "At least this foil will make some nice armor."

Finley unwrapped the gorp and poured it into Olivia's toiletry kit. Then she straightened out the foil and folded it around Olivia's neck. "How's that?"

"Good," said Olivia. "But what about you?"

"I'll be okay," said Finley. "I ate lots of garlic bread. They say it still works even after you brush your teeth." She blew out a noisy breath. "Take that, Dracumunk!" She grabbed the glow sticks. "You know what else vampires hate?"

"Light!" Olivia exclaimed.

"Exactly." Finley opened the package and passed Olivia a handful. They bent the glow sticks back and forth to activate them, then Finley took the lid off Olivia's water bottle and dropped a few in. The water lit up with neon rainbow colors.

"Okay," Finley said, handing the homemade glow lantern to Olivia, "now to find our way back. These smaller trails must hook up with the main trail at some point. But we've got to figure out some way to make sure we're not walking in circles." She started to put the extra glow sticks away.

"Hold on," said Olivia. "What about those? We could use them to mark the trails. That way we'll know which paths we've already tried."

"Brilliant!" said Finley. "Except that would be littering . . . "

"We could pick them up tomorrow when we hike," Olivia said.

"Perfect," Finley agreed, passing her some glow sticks.

Finley and Olivia slunk down the path. They placed the glow sticks every fifty steps and at every fork in the trail. Eventually, they came to a place where the trail made a *V*, but the right-hand path was already marked.

"Aha!" Finley cried. "Left it is!"

They followed the trail until it dead-ended, intersecting with a wider one.

"The main trail!" said Olivia. "But which way is the campsite — right or left?"

"We've got a fifty-fifty chance," said Finley. "Wanna do eenie meenie?"

Olivia looked both ways. "Wait! Remember when we were walking to the nature center and our shadows were in front of us?"

Finley nodded. "Uh-huh."

"If they were in front of us while we were walking *to* the nature center, and the moon hasn't moved that much since, then they should be *behind* us on the way back, right?" Olivia said.

Finley lit up. "Right!" Suddenly, she heard a noise.

CHIIICK-A-CHUCK. CHICK-CHIIICK.

Finley readied her slingshot and shield.

Olivia wielded her water gun. "Where is it coming from?" she whispered, her eyes darting from tree to tree.

CHIIICK-A-CHUCK. CHICK-CHIIICK.

Olivia lifted the lantern. Then she froze.

BLACK BERRY
CAMPSITE

Right beside them was a sign that read "Blackberry Campsite" with an arrow pointing left. On top of the sign sat a chubby-cheeked, beady-eyed chipmunk.

"Ruuuun!" Olivia squealed.

Chapter 10
TOUGH ENOUGH

Finley and Olivia tore down the trail and back to the campsite. They vaulted into the tent, and Finley zipped it up behind them.

"We made it!" Finley said, hugging her backpack. "We-made-it-we-made-it-we-made-it-we-made-it."

They lay on their backs, panting.

"Do you think anyone noticed we were gone?" Olivia whispered.

They sat up and held their breath. The only noise was a raspy, rumbling snore from the direction of the counselors' tent.

"Nope," said Finley. "Still snoring. I think this is something we should keep to ourselves."

"Deal," said Olivia. "What about our sleeping bags? Should we sneak out and get them?"

"No way," said Finley. "I'm not leaving this tent again until the sun's up."

Olivia lay back down on the cold, hard ground. "We don't need them," she said. "We're tough."

Yep, thought Finley. *But unfortunately, no one will ever know.*

* * *

The next morning, Finley awoke to Sunny's cheery voice. "Gi-iiirls! Time for breakfast!"

Finley rolled over and bumped into Olivia.

Olivia groaned. Her hair was matted, her face was smeared with sunscreen, and her bowl-helmet was still taped to her head. "Ugh," she croaked, opening her eyes.

Finley scratched her ankles and inspected them for bites. "Well, Dracumunk didn't get me, but the mosquitoes sure did."

"At least we're alive," said Olivia, giving her a limp fist bump.

"All right, girls, up and at 'em!" Sunny called. "We need to pack up before our morning hike. Remember the most important rule of camping — leave no trace." She unzipped the tent and poked her head in. "What happened to you two?"

Finley rolled over fast, and Olivia dove under a pile of clothes.

"Um . . . what do you mean?" Finley asked.

"I thought you were going to sleep under the stars," Sunny said.

"Oh," said Finley. "We were, but . . ."

"I chickened out," Olivia called from her hiding place. "Too many mosquitoes."

Sunny laughed. "You girls need to toughen up. You can't let a few mosquitoes keep you from having an adventure."

* * *

After the group packed up camp, they set out on their hike. Finley and Olivia took the lead.

"Don't get too far ahead!" Sunny called. "We wouldn't want you getting lost!"

"If she only knew," Finley mumbled.

When they reached the place where the main trail branched off, Finley spotted a glow stick down one of the paths. They were headed in that direction when Zoey yelled, "Other way, girls!"

"Maybe we could take this trail instead!" Olivia suggested.

"It *is* a beautiful trail," Sunny said, looking at her watch. "And we have just enough time before we have to get back for Field Day. Lead on!"

Finley and Olivia ran ahead, picking up glow sticks and shoving them into their pockets as they went.

"I think we got them all," Finley said as the end of the trail came into view. "Mission accomplished."

Chapter 11
THREE-LEGGED MESS

Back at Camp Acorn, Finley and Olivia headed to their cabin to get cleaned up. Then they met Henry, Kate, and Lia for a quick lunch before running to the message board to check the Field Day schedule.

"Looks like the three-legged race is first," said Lia.

Olivia glanced at Finley. "Want to try it?"

"Really?" Finley said doubtfully. Three-legged races didn't seem like Olivia's thing. But then again, neither did outsmarting and outrunning vampire chipmunks.

Henry looked surprised, too. Finley and Olivia didn't usually pair up for fun. "Do it!" he said. "I'll cheer for you!"

"We wouldn't stand a chance against the Saplings," Finley said.

"We won't know until we try," said Olivia. "Besides, we ran pretty fast last night," she added under her breath.

Finley thought about Zack — he wouldn't miss a chance to compete. "It's worth a try," she said. "But we'd better hurry. It starts in fifteen minutes."

After Finley and Olivia had signed up, Sunny handed them a thick strip of blue cloth. "All right, blue team, tie your ankles together," she said.

"Yikes." Finley nodded toward the other teams. "Some of those kids are twice as big as us."

"Remember Rocket from the Crawdad Derby?" said Henry. "Sometimes the smallest are the fastest."

"Good point," Finley said. She and Olivia tied their ankles together and took their place at the starting line. "Hey, I've got an idea. Let's pretend Dracumunk is right behind us!"

Olivia laughed. "That just might work."

Finley peered down the long line of competitors and spotted Zack at the end of the row. He was crouched next to his partner, tying a green strip of cloth around their ankles. No matter what Finley did, Zack would always be the oldest. But he didn't have to be first at everything.

Finley turned to Olivia. "Okay, Lightning Legs," she said. "Let's rock this race."

Sunny walked across the field with a megaphone. "Toes behind the line," she called out. "Izzy, tie your shoes. Spread out, make some room . . ." When she got to the far end, Sunny held the Camp Acorn flag above her head. "TEAMS, GET READY . . ." she bellowed into the megaphone. "SET . . ."

Finley bent down and put her hands on her knees, ready to spring.

"GO!"

At Sunny's signal, the teams surged forward. Finley tried to move quickly, but it seemed like every time her foot was up, Olivia's was down. "We're too far apart," she said, slipping her arm through Olivia's and pulling her closer.

The grass was soaked from the Saplings' morning sponge-tag game, and Finley and Olivia's feet made *splooshy* sounds each time they stepped. Some of the other teams, including Zack's, were already approaching the halfway mark.

Finley stumbled, but Olivia caught her by the elbow and pulled her up. "We've got to get a rhythm," Olivia said, "or we're going to fall."

Suddenly, Finley had an idea. "Down by the banks of the Hanky Panky, where the bullfrogs jump from bank to banky . . ." she chanted.

Olivia joined in. "With an eeps, ipes, opes, opps. One fell in and went kerplops!"

The girls marched in unison, stepping to the beat.

"We need more speed!" Olivia said, quickening the pace.

Before long, Finley and Olivia had caught up to the orange team and were neck and neck with the yellow and red teams as they rounded the halfway cone. The green team was in the lead, but the gap was closing. Zack was starting to drag his feet, and his partner's lanky legs had slowed to a walk.

The boys on the yellow team glanced over at Finley and Olivia. As they were gawking, the taller one tripped, and they both went down in a tangle of arms and legs, taking the red team with them.

"Kerplops!" Finley exclaimed as they blazed past the orange team. She set her eyes on the finish line. If they could just hang on a bit longer . . .

As they neared the end, the green team was struggling. The girls were gaining on them.

Finley gave Olivia a sideways glance.

Olivia nodded, and they took off running.

They caught up to Zack and his partner with only a few steps to go. But just when Finley thought they might actually have a chance, she slipped and pitched forward. Suddenly, she was sailing through the air, and Olivia was right beside her.

In that split second, Finley did the only thing she could do — she stretched out her arms and aimed for the finish line.

She landed with a thud, sending a splash of muddy water onto the spectators.

The crowd clapped and cheered, but when Finley looked up, her fingers were inches from the line. "Ugh," she groaned.

"Yes!" Henry's voice rang out.

Finley glanced over at Olivia, and a smile spread across her face. Olivia's hair was dripping dirty water. Her whole body was spattered with mud. But her right hand was over the line!

"AND THE BLUE TEAM WINS!" Sunny shouted through her megaphone. "WHAT A FINISH!"

"We did it!" Olivia cried.

Finley and Olivia peeled themselves off the ground and untied their ankles. Olivia started trying to wipe the mud off her shirt.

"It's okay," said Finley. "It makes you look tough."

"I *am* tough," Olivia said.

Finley grinned. "Come on."

As they left the field, Henry, Kate, and Lia came running up.

"You guys were amazing!" Henry said.

"Thanks," Finley and Olivia said together.

"Hey!" someone shouted after them.

Finley recognized Zack's voice and spun around.

"Not bad," her brother said as he ambled up.

Finley waited for him to add "for a girl," but he didn't.

"You dominated that race," Zack said, giving Finley and Olivia each a fist bump. "You're tougher than I thought. But you two better watch out next year — I'm going to start training tomorrow."

As Zack ran off to catch up to his buddies, something fell out of his pocket. Finley picked it up and jogged after him. It was a wooden letter *B*. By the looks of it, he'd whittled it himself. "Zack!" she called. "You dropped something."

Zack sprinted back. "Shhh!" he said, grabbing it out of her hand.

"Why?" Finley asked. "What is it?"

"Keep it down," he whispered hoarsely.

Just then someone yelled, "Bree!" and a Sapling girl with bobbed hair and freckles bounded by. Zack's head swiveled in her direction.

Finley followed Zack's gaze. "*B* for Bree?" she guessed.

Zack's cheeks turned tomato red.

"Is that your *girlfriend*?" Finley's eyes widened.

"Enough with the questions," Zack said. "Yes, B is for Bree, and no, she's not my girlfriend. We're friends. I was going to give this to her, but I changed my mind."

"Why?" Finley asked.

Zack shrugged. "I don't think she'd like it."

"*I* think you're *scared*," Finley said. "Of a *girl!*"

Zack frowned. "Look, just forget it, okay? Maybe I will give it to her, maybe I won't — I don't know."

"You should," said Finley. "It's nice." She pulled some leather lacing out of her pocket. "Here. You can put it on this. It's leftover from my ninja nunchuks. If you're too scared to give it to her, *I'll* do it for you."

Zack stuffed the lacing into his pocket. "*No*, you won't. And don't say a word. Or else —"

Just then, Henry and Olivia caught up to them, and Zack quickly shut his mouth. He gave Finley a final warning glance before dashing off after his friends.

"You look like you had a mud bath!" Henry said.

Finley grinned. "It's war paint." She skimmed some mud off her shorts and held up a finger. "Want some?"

"Sure," said Henry.

Finley smeared lines on Henry's cheeks.

"How do I look?" Henry asked, making a face.

"Fierce," Finley told him.

Olivia nodded. "You're gonna rule the egg toss. Hey, want to swing by the snack station? I could go for some gorp."

"Okay," said Finley. "You pick out the chocolate chips, and we'll eat the rest."

As they headed for the picnic tables, Sunny stopped them. "Hold it right there," she said. "You forgot your ribbons. And I need a picture." She handed Finley and Olivia each a satiny blue ribbon, and they stood beside Henry.

"All right," said Sunny. "Say mu-uuud!"

"Mu-uuud!" they all shouted.

Sunny snapped the picture. "Way to go, girls! You may be messy, but when it comes to three-legged races, you don't mess around!"

Chapter 12
JAR FULL OF MEMORIES

That night, all the campers and counselors gathered for a bonfire. When Finley and Olivia arrived, Lia and Kate were playing charades with their cabin counselor while Henry and the rest of the camp cooking crew were wrapping up foil packages and setting them in the coals.

"What are those?" Finley asked.

"Banana boats," Henry said. "You're gonna love them."

After a few minutes, Doc fished the packets out of the fire and laid them on the picnic table to cool. Henry slid one onto a paper plate and carefully pulled the foil apart, letting out a wisp of sweet-smelling steam. "Try it," he said, handing Finley a spoon. "It's like a hot banana split."

Finley dug into the baked banana and melted chocolate-marshmallow mixture. "Mmmm . . ." she said, her mouth full of marshmallow. "This is the yummiest thing yet."

"I might actually miss some of the camp cooking," said Olivia.

"Me, too," said Henry. "Mom's going to have to fire up the grill so we can try it at home."

Finley leaned back to watch the sunset. The clouds were big and billowy — her favorite kind — in a rainbow of cotton-candy colors. "I can't believe the week went by so fast," she said. "I'm going to miss everything about camp — the sunsets, the Craft Raft, the creek . . ."

"The mosquitoes?" said Olivia.

Finley laughed. "Okay, *almost* everything."

"I'm sure they'll miss you," said Henry. "Well, only the females — the males feed on flower nectar. I read it in my bug book."

Just then Sunny stood on one of the benches and blew her whistle. "Attention, campers!" she called. "We hope you've enjoyed your week at Camp Acorn and that you'll take home lots of happy memories. The counselors are coming around with your memory jars to fill with souvenirs from your time here. If you haven't collected any keepsakes, it's not too late."

"Hey, do you guys have anything for your jars?" Olivia asked.

"Uh-oh," said Finley. "I totally forgot."

"I have a few things," said Henry. "We can share them if you want."

"Thanks," said Olivia. "Maybe Finley and I can gather some stuff, too."

"Sounds good," said Finley. "Meet back here in fifteen minutes."

* * *

When they got back, Finley, Henry, and Olivia spread their treasures out on the picnic table and surveyed the collection.

Henry had brought his notebook and was busy writing out the banana boat recipe and copies of his "Best Things about Camp Acorn" list for Finley and Olivia.

"Maybe we can ask Sunny for a copy of that picture she took after the race," Olivia said, passing Finley a glow stick.

"Why an old glow stick?" Henry asked.

Olivia looked at Finley and winked. "A reminder of our campout adventure."

"Here," said Finley, handing Olivia some ninja throwing stars. "I made them in camp crafts. They're great for vampire chipmunks."

Olivia gave her a secret smile. "Thanks," she said.

"And this is for you," Finley said to Henry, dangling her present in front of his face. "I knitted you a fish! It's a rainbow trout. I wanted to make it bigger, but I ran out of yarn."

"Aw, thanks." Henry grinned. "It's bigger than any fish *I'll* ever catch."

"Not true," said Finley. "But it's a lot less stinky."

Finley opened her memory jar and dropped in a throwing star, a fuzzy piece of yarn, a smooth rock from Crawdad

Creek, Henry's recipe and list, some acorns for her slingshot, and her first place ribbon from the three-legged race. "Ta-daah!" she said, holding it up. "Camp Acorn in a jar!"

* * *

The next morning, after end-of-the-week tidy time, Henry, Finley, and Olivia hiked to the creek. They sat with their feet in the water, throwing in twigs and leaves and watching them float away.

Finley took a deep breath. The air smelled like earth and growing things. "I wonder where Lightning Legs is?" she said, her eyes searching the shallows.

"Hiding," said Henry. "She probably saw us coming."

"You know, crawdads *are* kind of cute once you get used to them," said Olivia.

"Don't even think about it," said Henry. "Crawdads are *not* pets."

Finley made finger-claws at Olivia. "I've heard there's a zombie crawdad that lives in this very creek."

"Okay, okay," Olivia said with a laugh. "I'll stick to stuffed animals."

Henry sighed. "I can't believe I didn't catch a single fish this whole week."

"There's always next year," said Finley. "Maybe I'll knit you a net."

Olivia cupped her hand and dipped it into the creek, then let the water trickle through her fingers. "You know, camp wasn't as bad as I thought it would be. I did more than survive — I had fun. Maybe I'll come back next year, too."

"You'd better," said Finley, smiling. "I'll need a partner for the three-legged race."

* * *

When Finley's mom and Evie arrived to pick them up, Finley and Henry said their goodbyes and went to the office to meet Zack and check out. While they were waiting, Finley glanced at the photo wall.

"Look!" she said, pointing. Right in the middle was the photo of her, Olivia, and Henry. They were covered in mud and grinning.

"Wow!" Evie said. "You guys are really dirty!"

Just then Zack came jogging up. "Sorry I'm late," he said. "I was saying goodbye." His eyes met Finley's, and he gave her a thumbs-up.

"*B?*" she mouthed.

Zack smiled, his cheeks turning pink.

As they walked to the car, Finley spotted Kate, Lia, and Olivia doing cartwheels in the field.

"Bye!" Finley yelled. "Have a great time at your grandma's, Olivia! Eat a brownie for me!"

"I will!" Olivia shouted back. "See you at school!"

Sunny and Doc waved as the car pulled away.

"Until next time," Sunny called, "peace, love, and crawdads!"

Finley, Henry, and Zack waved back. "Peace, love, and crawdads!"

As the car bounced along the gravel road, it occurred to Finley there were all kinds of tough. Zack was like a crawdad — tough on the outside. Henry was a quieter kind of tough, the kind that never gave up. Then there was be-yourself tough. Olivia was like

that. She did things her way and didn't care what other people thought.

What kind of tough am I? Finley wondered. She watched the trees swaying back and forth in the breeze, waving goodbye with their branches. Maybe she was like a tree — the flexible kind of tough. When she had a problem, she thought of lots of different ways to solve it. She bent this way and that, but she didn't break.

Mom glanced in the rearview mirror. "So . . . tell me all about it. How was Camp Acorn?" she asked.

Finley looked at her memory jar and smiled. "Fin-tastic," she said.

About the Author

Jessica Young grew up in Ontario, Canada. The same things make her happy now as when she was a kid: dancing, painting, music, digging in the dirt, picnics, reading, and writing. Like Finley Flowers, Jessica loves making stuff. When she was little, she wanted to be a tap-dancing flight attendant/ veterinarian, but she's changed her mind! Jessica currently lives with her family in Nashville, Tennessee.

About the Illustrator

When Jessica Secheret was young, she had strange friends that were always with her: felt pens, colored pencils, brushes, and paint. After repainting all the walls in her house, her parents decided it was time for her to express her "talent" at an art school — the famous École Boulle in Paris. After several years at various architecture agencies, Jessica decided to give up squares, rulers, and compasses and dedicate her heart and soul to what she'd always loved — putting her own imagination on paper. Today, Jessica spends her time in her Paris studio, drawing for magazines and children's books in France and abroad.

Henry's Gorp

Ask an adult to supervise, and have fun making some of Finley's and Henry's creations!

What You'll Need:

1 cup peanuts
1 cup raisins or dried cranberries
1 cup chocolate chips
1 cup granola cereal, optional

What to Do:

Mix all the above ingredients together and enjoy! Separate your gorp into individual bags to take on your next adventure as a healthy snack. You can also create your own variations on this classic camp snack by adding dried pineapple, banana chips, dried apricots, almonds, pretzels, or yogurt-covered raisins. And remember — don't feed the chipmuuunksssss . . .

Camp Acorn Banana Boats

* Be safe and have an adult do the baking and cutting for you. Never touch an oven!

What You'll Need:

1 unpeeled banana per person (unless you want to share)
Chocolate chips
Mini marshmallows
Aluminum foil

What to Do:

Make a lengthwise slit down each banana. Pull the banana open slightly and stuff with chocolate chips and mini marshmallows. Wrap tightly with foil, and bake at 300 degrees for 15 minutes, or until chocolate and marshmallows are melted and banana is warm. Have an adult pull back the foil and let cool a bit before serving. Get a spoon and dig in!